Boudreaux the Louisiana Mosquiteaux

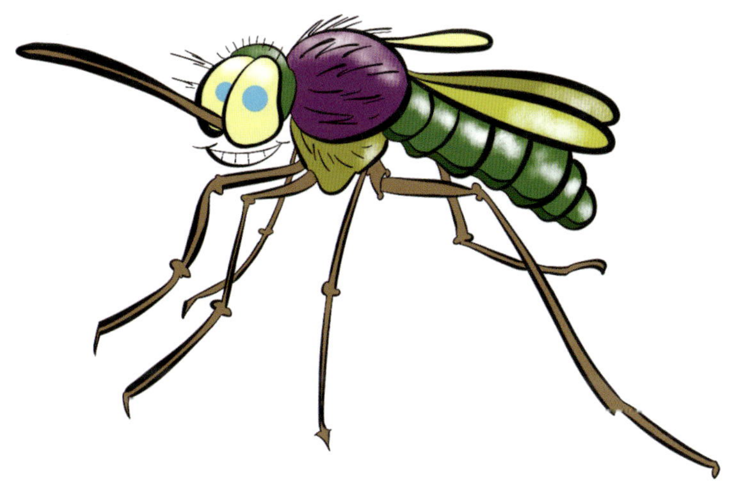

Written and Illustrated by
Stacy Bearden

ISBN: 9781455622474
Ebook ISBN: 9781455622481

Printed in China

Published by Pelican Publishing
New Orleans, Louisiana
www.pelicanpub.com

For Ethan and Madeline

Boudreaux the Mosquiteaux was a baby mosquito. Just after he hatched, a big hurricane swept him away in a gust of wind. Little Boudreaux did not even have time for his first breakfast, and he was very hungry.

"Maybe I can ask other animals to help me find breakfast!" he thought. Boudreaux spotted an animal at the edge of the swamp.

"Mr. Alligator, I am hungry. What do I eat?" asked Boudreaux.

"I eat fish. Go ask the wolf," answered the alligator.

So Boudreaux flew away to find the wolf.

"Mr. Wolf, I am hungry. What do I eat?" asked Boudreaux.

"I eat rabbits. Go ask the bear," answered the wolf.

So Boudreaux flew away to find the bear.

“Mr. Bear, I am hungry. What do I eat?” asked Boudreaux.

“I eat honey. Go ask the wild hog,” answered the bear.

So Boudreaux flew away to find the wild hog.

"Ms. Hog, I am hungry. What do I eat?" asked Boudreaux.

"I eat roots. Go ask the snake," answered the wild hog.

So Boudreaux flew away to find the snake.

"Mr. Snake, I am hungry. What do I eat?" asked Boudreaux.

"I eat ratssss. Go assssk the armadillo," answered the snake.

So Boudreaux flew away to find the armadillo.

“Ms. Armadillo, I am hungry. What do I eat?” asked Boudreaux.

“I eat ants. Go ask the raccoons,” answered the armadillo.

So Boudreaux flew away to find the raccoons.

“Mr. and Mrs. Raccoon, I am hungry. What do I eat?” asked Boudreaux.

“We eat fruit. Go ask the owl,” answered the raccoons.

So Boudreaux flew away to find the owl.

"Mr. Owl, I am hungry. What do I eat?" asked Boudreaux.

"I eat birds. Go ask the opossum," answered the owl.

So Boudreaux flew away to find the opossum.

"Ms. Opossum, I am hungry. What do I eat?" asked Boudreaux.

"I eat frogs. Go ask the catfish," answered the opossum.

So Boudreaux flew away to find the catfish.

"Mr. Catfish, I am hungry. What do I eat?" asked Boudreaux.

"I eat worms. Go ask the frog," answered the catfish.

So Boudreaux flew away to find the frog.

“Mr. Frog, I am hungry. What do I eat?” asked Boudreaux.

“I eat flies. Go ask the egret,” answered the frog.

So Boudreaux flew away to find the egret.

"Ms. Egret, I am hungry. What do I eat?" asked Boudreaux.

"I eat shrimp. Go ask the cardinal," answered the egret.

So Boudreaux flew away to find the cardinal.

"Mr. Cardinal, I am hungry. What do I eat?" asked Boudreaux.

"I eat seeds. Go ask the turtle," answered the cardinal.

So Boudreaux flew away to find the turtle.

"Mr. Turtle, I am hungry. What do I eat?" asked Boudreaux.

"I eat bugs. Go ask the pelicans," answered the turtle.

So Boudreaux flew away to find the pelicans.

"Mr. and Mrs. Pelican, I am hungry. What do I eat?" asked Boudreaux.

"We eat fish. Go ask the crawfish," answered the pelicans.

So Boudreaux flew away to find the crawfish. He thought the animals were not being very helpful. . . .

“Mr. Crawfish, I am hungry. What do I eat?” asked Boudreaux.

“I eat rice. Go ask the squirrel,” answered the crawfish.

So Boudreaux flew away to find the squirrel.

"Mr. Squirrel, I am hungry. What do I eat?" asked Boudreaux.

"I eat acorns. Go ask the fawn," answered the squirrel.

So Boudreaux flew away to find the fawn.

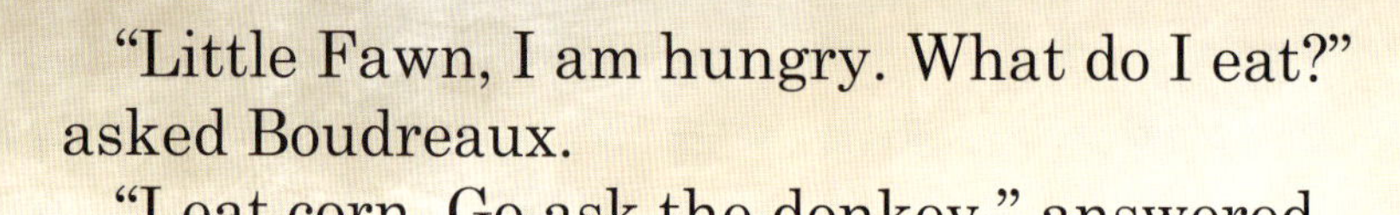

"Little Fawn, I am hungry. What do I eat?" asked Boudreaux.

"I eat corn. Go ask the donkey," answered the fawn.

So Boudreaux flew away to find the donkey.

"Mr. Donkey, I am hungry. What do I eat?" asked Boudreaux.

"Heehaw! Heehaw!" brayed the donkey loudly.

"How dare you!" replied Boudreaux, and he flew away to find some better help. At the edge of a farm, he spotted two goats.

"Little Goat, I am hungry. What do I eat?" asked Boudreaux.

"I eat anything! Go ask the bumblebee," answered the little goat.

So Boudreaux flew away to find the bumblebee.

“Mr. Bumblebee, I am hungry. What do I eat?” asked Boudreaux.

“I eat nectar. Go ask the duckling,” answered the bumblebee.

So Boudreaux flew away to find the duckling.

"Little Duckling, I am hungry. What do I eat?" asked Boudreaux.

"I eat grass. Go ask the kitten," answered the duckling.

So Boudreaux flew into a yard to find the kitten.

"Little Kitten, I am hungry. What do I eat?" asked Boudreaux.

"I drink my mother's milk. Go ask the hound dog," answered the kitten.

So Boudreaux flew up to the porch to find the hound dog.

"Mr. Hound Dog, I am hungry. What do I eat?" asked Boudreaux.

"Little Mosquito, you don't know what you eat? *Mon ami,* you eat Cajuns! There is one right over there." The hound dog pointed behind him with his scruffy tail.

Boudreaux the Mosquiteaux quickly flew to the Cajun and landed on his arm. Little Boudreaux was hungry! He had missed breakfast, and now it was lunch.

"I can finally eat!" said Boudreaux. . . .

WHACK

The End.

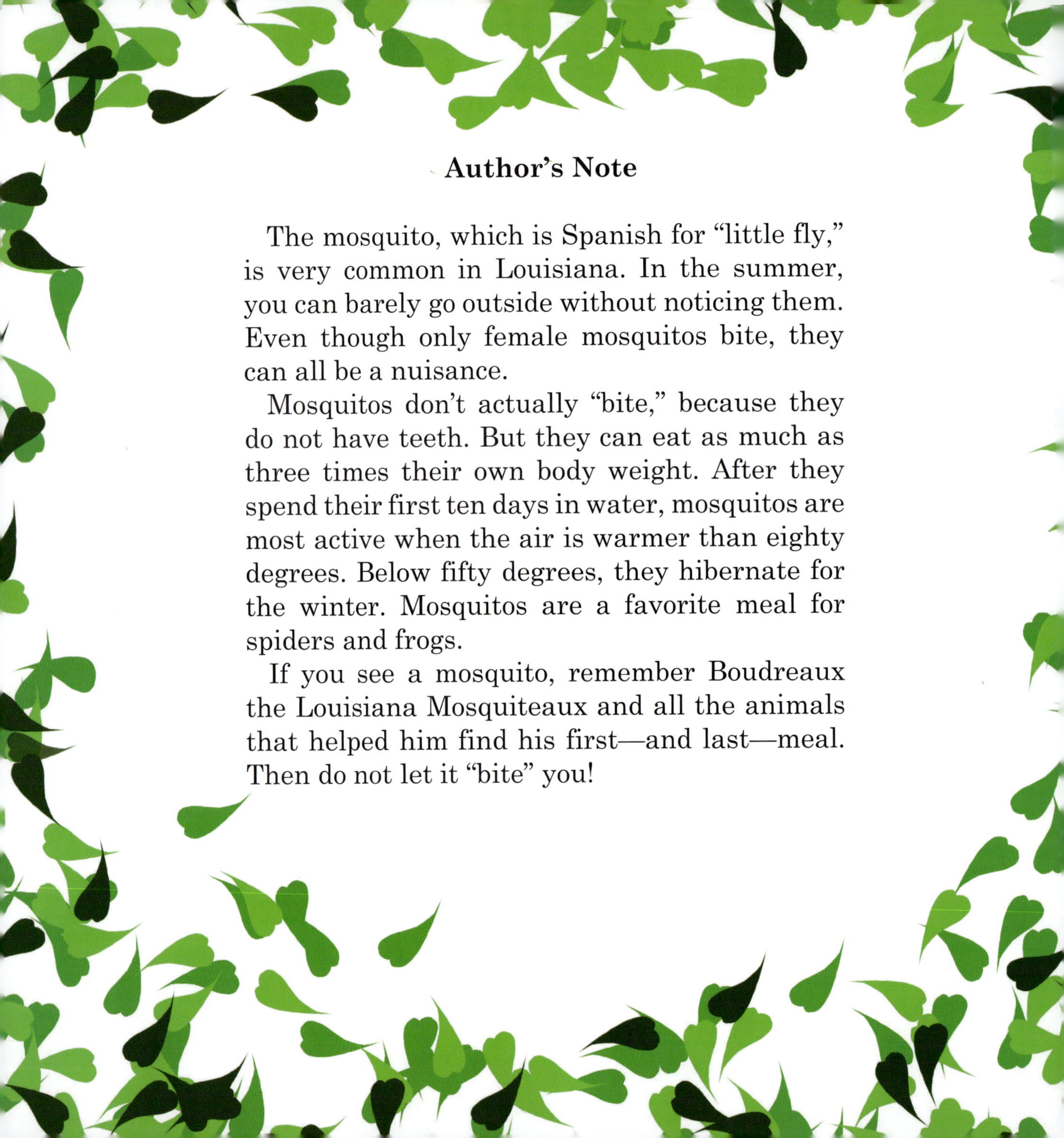

Author's Note

The mosquito, which is Spanish for "little fly," is very common in Louisiana. In the summer, you can barely go outside without noticing them. Even though only female mosquitos bite, they can all be a nuisance.

Mosquitos don't actually "bite," because they do not have teeth. But they can eat as much as three times their own body weight. After they spend their first ten days in water, mosquitos are most active when the air is warmer than eighty degrees. Below fifty degrees, they hibernate for the winter. Mosquitos are a favorite meal for spiders and frogs.

If you see a mosquito, remember Boudreaux the Louisiana Mosquiteaux and all the animals that helped him find his first—and last—meal. Then do not let it "bite" you!